EARLY BIRD
STORIES

Look Out!
&
Dot and Dan's Trip

Early ★ Reader

First American edition published in 2023 by Lerner Publishing Group, Inc.

An original concept by Katie Dale
Copyright © 2023 Katie Dale

Illustrated by Dean Gray

First published by Maverick Arts Publishing Limited

Maverick
arts publishing

Licensed Edition
Look Out! & Dan and Dot's Trip

Lerner Publications Company
An imprint of Lerner Publishing Group, Inc.
241 First Avenue North
Minneapolis, MN 55401 USA

For reading levels and more information, look up this title at www.lernerbooks.com.

Main body text set in Mikado a. Typeface provided by HVD Fonts.

Library of Congress Cataloging-in-Publication Data

Names: Dale, Katie, author. | Gray, Dean, illustrator. | Dale, Katie. Look out! | Dale, Katie. Dot and Dan's trip.
Title: Look out! ; & Dot and Dan's trip / Katie Dale ; illustrated by Dean Gray.
Other titles: Look out! (Compilation)
Description: First American edition. | Minneapolis : Lerner Publications, [2023] | Series: Early bird readers. Pink (Early bird stories) | "First published by Maverick Arts Publishing Limited"—Page facing title page. | Audience: Ages 4–8. | Audience: Grades K–1. | Summary: "Dot and Dan are two mice trying to get some cheese. Will they get it? Then the pair go on a trip. Will there be cheese on their trip?"— Provided by publisher.
Identifiers: LCCN 2022020163 | ISBN 9781728476421 (lib. bdg.) | ISBN 9781728478463 (pbk.) | ISBN 9781728482149 (eb pdf)
Subjects: LCSH: Readers (Primary) | LCGFT: Readers (Publications)
Classification: LCC PE1119.2 .D3524 2023 | DDC 428.6/2—dc23/eng/20220510

LC record available at https://lccn.loc.gov/2022020163

Manufactured in the United States of America
1-52223-50663-6/20/2022

EARLY BIRD STORIES

Look Out!
&
Dot and Dan's Trip

Katie Dale

Illustrated by
Dean Gray

Lerner Publications ◆ Minneapolis

The Letter "T"

Trace the lower and upper case letter with a finger. Sound out the letter.

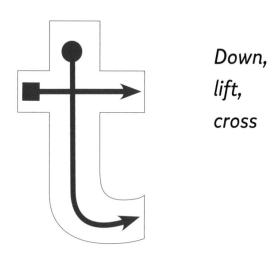

*Down,
lift,
cross*

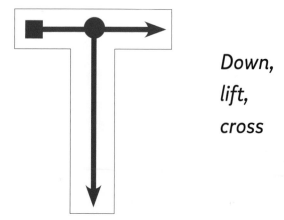

*Down,
lift,
cross*

Some words to familiarize:

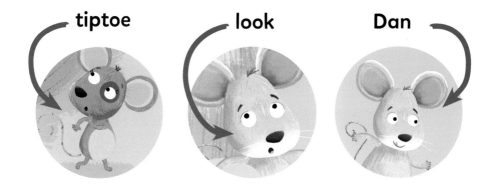

tiptoe   look   Dan

High-frequency words:

the

Tips for Reading *Look Out!*

- Practice the words listed above before reading the story.

- If the reader struggles with any of the other words, ask them to look for sounds they know in the word. Encourage them to sound out the words and help them read the words if necessary.

- After reading the story, ask the reader what happens to the cat in the end.

Fun Activity

Discuss what Dot and Dan will have to look out for next time.

Look Out!

Tiptoe past the bed.

Look out, Dan!

Tiptoe past the mug.

Look out, Dan!

Tiptoe past the cat.

Look out, Dan!

Tiptoe past the mop.

Look out, Dan!

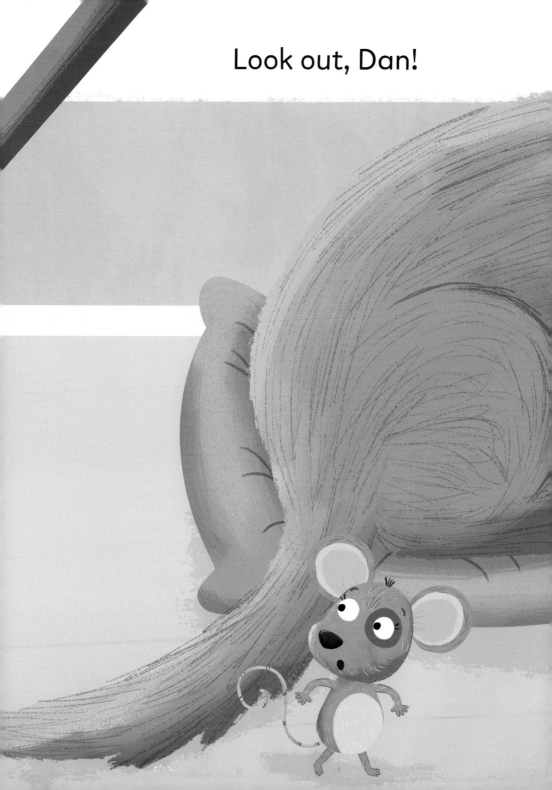

Tiptoe past the dog.

Look out, Dan!

Look out, cat!

The Letter "D"

Trace the lower and upper case letter with a finger. Sound out the letter.

Around,
up,
down

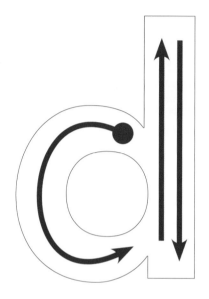

Down,
up,
around

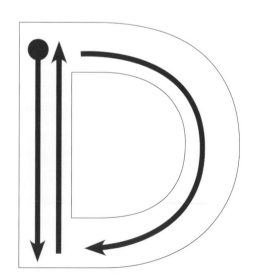

Some words to familiarize:

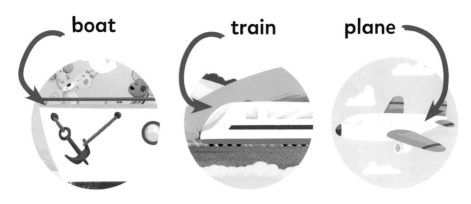

boat   **train**   **plane**

High-frequency words:

a   go   on

Tips for Reading *Dot and Dan's Trip*

- Practice the words listed above before reading the story.

- If the reader struggles with any of the other words, ask them to look for sounds they know in the word. Encourage them to sound out the words and help them read the words if necessary.

- After reading the story, ask the reader how Dan kept losing his cheese.

Fun Activity

Discuss why Dan is so happy to be home.

Dot and Dan's Trip

Dot and Dan go on a bus.

Dot and Dan go on a boat.

Dot and Dan go on a plane.

Dot and Dan go on a train.

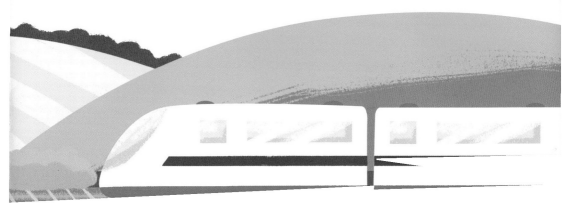

Dot and Dan go on a car.

COLOR		GRL
Silver	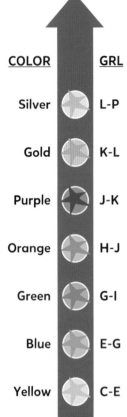	L-P
Gold		K-L
Purple		J-K
Orange		H-J
Green		G-I
Blue		E-G
Yellow		C-E
Red		C-D
Pink		A-C

Leveled for Guided Reading

Early Bird Stories have been edited and leveled by leading educational consultants to correspond with guided reading levels. The levels are assigned by taking into account the content, language style, layout, and phonics used in each book. Visit www.lernerbooks.com for more Early Bird Readers titles!